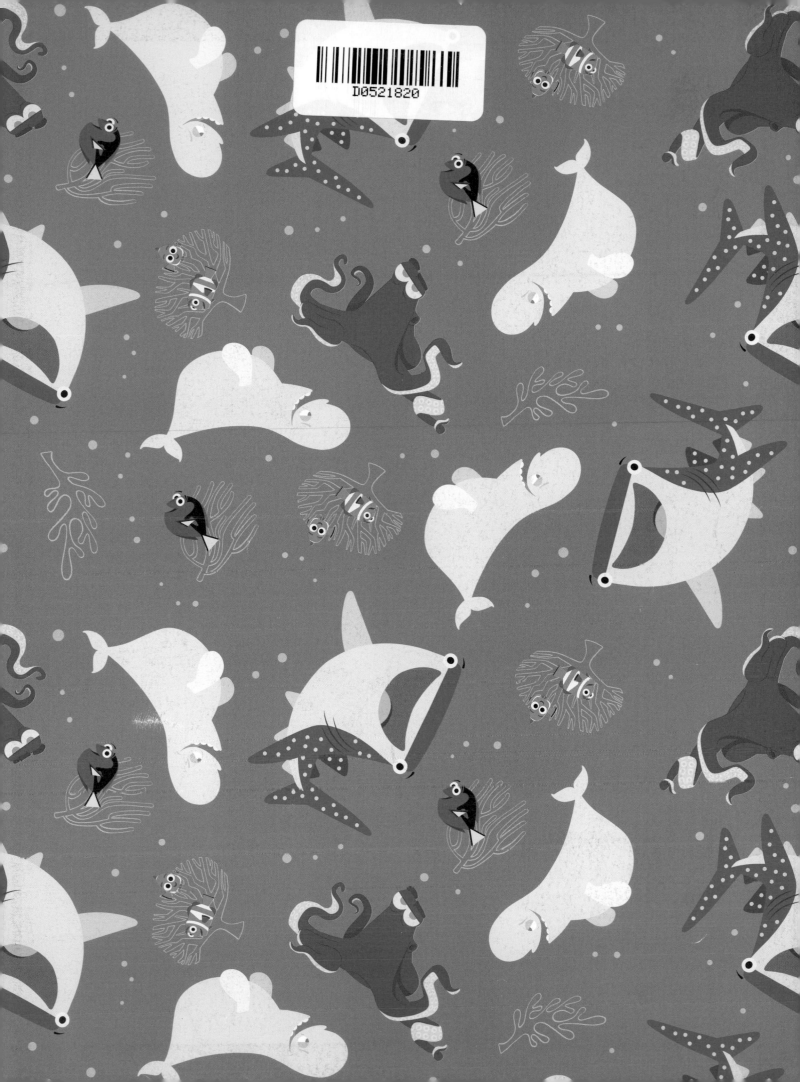

EGMONT
We bring stories to life

First published in 2016 by Egmont UK Limited,
The Yellow Building, 1 Nicholas Road, London W11 4AN

Activities and story adaptations by Catherine Shoolbred
Designed by Jeannette O'Toole

© 2016 Disney/Pixar

ISBN 978 1 4052 8343 4
63789/1
Printed in Italy

Stay safe online. Egmont is not responsible
for content hosted by third parties.

Disney · PIXAR
FINDING DORY

Annual 2017

This
Finding Dory Annual 2017
belongs to ...

Contents

FINDING DORY

Welcome to this fun, fish-filled annual! Find out how forgetful Dory starts remembering her past. Can she find her family?

Then read on to look back at when Dory helped Marlin find Nemo, and see the adventures they have with their ocean friends!

FINDING NEMO

Look out for this jellyfish. It's hidden 10 times in the annual.

ANSWER: the 10 jellyfish are hidden on pages 14, 18, 22, 29, 37, 40, 45, 48, 53 and 63.

Meet Dory & her Friends

A year after Marlin and Dory found Nemo, Dory starts remembering her past. Soon, they set off on another big adventure to find Dory's family!

Nemo and Marlin

Nemo lives on the coral reef with his dad, Marlin. But when Dory starts talking about her past, they agree to help her find her family.

Dory

Forgetful Dory is happy living on the coral reef with her friends, Marlin and Nemo, until she starts remembering her parents. Nemo and Marlin leave with her to look for her family, but they get separated and Dory ends up alone in the Marine Life Institute.

Jenny, Charlie and Baby Dory

As a baby, Dory lived with her parents, Jenny and Charlie, at the Marine Life Institute, the MLI. One day Dory disappeared and by the time grown-up Dory finds her way back to the MLI, her parents are no longer there.

Becky and Gerald

Becky, the loon, helps Marlin and Nemo get into the Marine Life Institute to look for Dory. She does this by carrying them there in Gerald the sea lion's favourite green bucket!

Bailey

This beluga whale came to the Marine Life Institute with a head injury. He thought his echolocation skill had been damaged and it's only when grown-up Dory returns to the MLI that he finally uses his ability again to help Dory find her family.

Hank

This seven-limbed octopus is a master of disguise and wants to escape the MLI. He helps Dory move around in water-filled items like a coffee jug and a child's sippy cup!

Destiny

This whale shark taught baby Dory to speak whale! Destiny is thrilled when grown-up Dory returns to the MLI. Dory inspires her to return to the ocean.

9

Finding Dory

Part 1

Enjoy the exciting story of the Finding Dory movie!

Dory has always had a bad memory. When she was little, she lived with her parents, who helped her with her memory, but one day she ended up alone in the ocean and she couldn't remember how she had got there.

Over the years Dory tried asking other fish for help, but they either ignored her or she forgot about them. It wasn't until she met Marlin and helped him find his son Nemo that she made some real friends.

One day Dory remembers her parents and 'the Jewel of Morro Bay', so Marlin and Nemo go there with her to find them. But when they arrive, Dory swims up to a friendly voice and is scooped up by people on a Marine Life Institute boat. They tag her and take her to the MLI aquarium.

There, Dory meets Hank the octopus, who agrees to help her if she'll give him her tag so he can go to the quieter Cleveland aquarium. Meanwhile, some sea lions tell Marlin and Nemo how they can get into the MLI to rescue Dory – they can be carried in by Becky, the loon, in Gerald the sea lion's green bucket!

In the Marine Life Institute, Dory meets Bailey and Destiny. She discovers that she had lived in the Open Ocean tank at the MLI when she was little, and it was Destiny who had taught her to speak 'whale'!

Knowing that her parents could be in the Open Ocean tank, Dory is desperate to go there, but she's too scared to go through the pipes. Hank agrees to take her there in a beaker on a pram!

The story continues on page 24 ...

What Comes Next?

Can you work out who comes next in each sequence?

1 ?

2 ?

3 ?

4 ?

Dory & Destiny

Destiny is thrilled to see Dory again! Add colour to show the happy friends together.

Sea Shadow Match

Draw lines to match these sea friends to their shadows.

1

2

3

4

a

b

c

d

Can you find 5 starfish hidden on the page? Trace over the number when you've found them all.

5

Fish Count

How many of each fish friend can you count?
Draw over the lines to add the numbers
in the shells below.

Marlin

Nemo

Dory

Bailey

Destiny

Maze Rescue

Dory has forgotten where she's going!
Which route does Nemo need to take
through the maze to find her?

1

2

3

Dory Dot-to-Dot

Join the dots then colour in Dory
so she can swim away.

4
25
22
24   3
5
1
2   6
21   23
7
18
8
9
20
19
10
15
16
11
17
14
13   12

19

Spot the Difference

These two seabed scenes look the same,
but there are 6 differences in picture 2.
Can you spot them all?

1

Colour in a seashell as you spot each difference.

2

ANSWER:

21

Sea Shape Sudoku

Can you draw these missing sea shapes in the grid?

TIP: Each image can only appear once in each row and column.

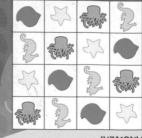

ANSWER:

Dory's Letters

Dory accidentally becomes Mr Ray's Teaching Assistant. She's trying to remember what type of creatures the friends below are. Help her by colouring in the letter that each creature begins with.

1

Hank the octopus

Z m o

2

Gerald the sea lion

s v n

3

Becky the loon

x l f

ANSWERS: 1. o for octopus, **2.** s for sea lion, **3.** l for loon.

23

Finding Dory

Part 2

Read on to enjoy the rest of the Finding Dory movie story!

Dory gives Hank her tag as he says goodbye and puts her into the Open Ocean tank. Dory spots a shell path that leads to her childhood home, but she's then told that her parents were moved to Quarantine. Bailey uses echolocation to guide Dory through the pipes to Quarantine.

Dory meets Marlin and Nemo in the pipes and they bump into Hank in the loading zone. He's about to be loaded onto a truck going to the Cleveland aquarium. There's a tank of blue tang fish going too, so Hank carries Marlin and Nemo to it, not realising that Dory's parents aren't there. As Hank goes to bring Dory to it too, he's picked up by a MLI worker, which makes him accidentally drop Dory down a drain. Dory ends up alone in the ocean again!

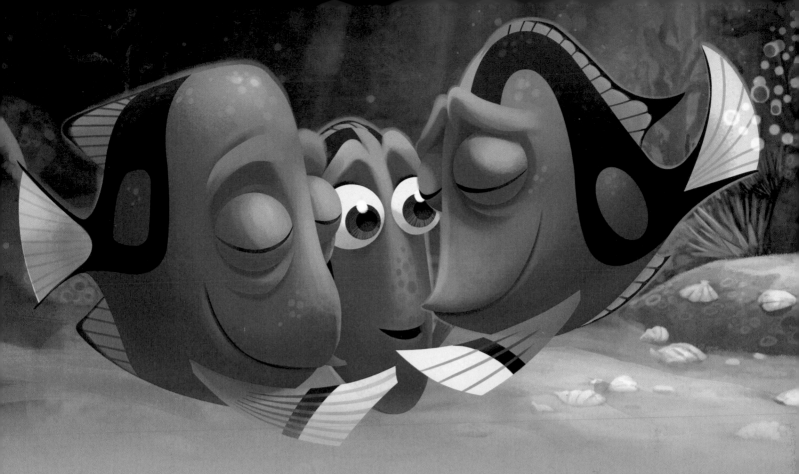

Dory thinks: 'What would Dory do?' which leads her to follow a trail of seashells along the seabed. Amazingly it leads to her parents, who had been waiting there for her all these years! Dory's thrilled to have found them, but she knows she must rescue Marlin and Nemo, who are now in the truck going to Cleveland! Bailey and Destiny jump into the ocean to help Dory.

Bailey uses echolocation to follow the truck. When it stops on a bridge, Dory asks some otters to take her up it and put her in the truck. When Destiny tells them that the traffic is moving again, Marlin calls Becky the loon for help.

Becky scoops up Marlin and Nemo in Gerald's bucket and carries them back to the ocean. But when she heads back for Dory, the MLI people shut the door, trapping Becky, Hank and Dory inside! Dory spots a roof vent and Hank carries her onto the roof. When he slides down the windscreen, the people in the van scream and run away. Hank slides into the driver's seat and puts Dory in a cup of water. He presses the accelerator, sending the truck careering along the road.

With the truck running out of petrol, Dory gets Hank to drive it off the bridge. As the truck flips over, the back doors open and all the sea creatures fall safely into the sea. Dory finally has everything she has ever wanted, her friends, both old and new, and her long-lost family all together at last!

THE END

Dory's Maze

Can you help Dory find her way through the maze to her parents?

START

FINISH

ANSWER:

Fishing Lines

Follow the fishing lines to see which one leads to each fish friend.

1 2 3

Bailey

Dory

Marlin

Odd Fish Out

Circle the picture in each line that's different from the rest.

1. a b c d

2. a b c d

3. a b c d

4. a b c d

Cheer Up Hank

Poor Hank is feeling sad. Cheer him up by using your brightest orange pens to colour him in.

Colourful Friends

Trace over the letters to write what colours these friends are.
Then colour in the paint splodges to match.

pink

grey

brown

blue

33

Biggest & Smallest

Add letters in the boxes to put the sea creatures in size order from the smallest to the biggest.

smallest ☐ ☐ ☐ ☐ ☐ biggest

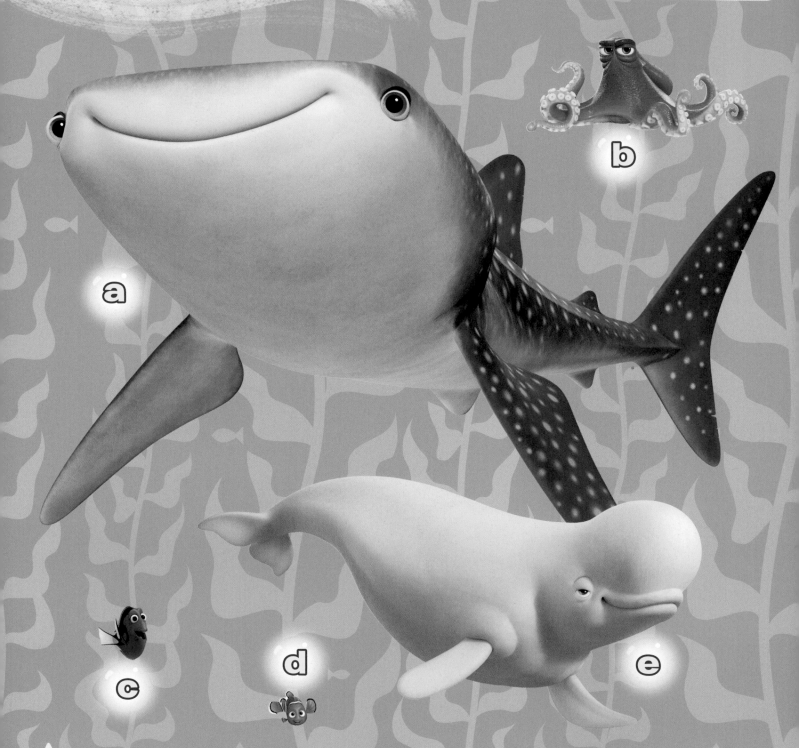

a

b

c

d

e

34

JUST KEEP SWIMMING!

NEVER forget your friends

CUT ALONG HERE

FINDING NEMO

A year before Dory's big adventure, Nemo has one of his own. His father, Marlin, was so busy keeping him safe that he didn't let Nemo have any fun. But when Nemo swam away from the coral reef, he was taken by a diver and put in a dentist's fish tank!

Despite her forgetfulness, Dory helps reunite Marlin with his son, Nemo. Before long they all settle into life on the ocean floor, where they meet new friends and have more fun and adventures along the way!

Are you ready for an adventure?

Meet Nemo & his Friends

Nemo and his dad, Marlin, made lots of friends on their ocean adventure.

Nemo
He's a brave little clownfish who loves exploring.

Marlin
Nemo's father tries to protect his curious son from danger.

Dory
This happy and helpful blue tang is very forgetful.

Crush and Squirt
These chilled out turtles love riding the East Australian current.

Bruce
He looks scary, but this shark's motto is that fish are friends, not food!

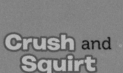

School Friends

Tad, Pearl and Sheldon are some of the
friends Nemo meets at Mr Ray's school.

Tad

Sheldon

Pearl

Gil

Bubbles

Bloat

The Tank Gang

help Nemo escape
the fish tank, so he can
find his father.

Gurgle

Deb & Flo

Peach

Jacques

Clowning Around

Add colour to this picture of Nemo and his Tank Gang pals playing a game.

How many arms does Peach, the starfish, have?

40

Great Escape

A year before Dory's search for her family, Nemo has his own big adventure ...

 lives with his father, , but

one day a diver takes and puts

him in a fish tank! hurries after

 with help from . As they

travel they make friends with sharks,

 rescues  from a jellyfish

field, they escape from a whale's

mouth, and swim with turtles along

the East Australian Current to Sydney.

When you see these pictures say their names out loud:

Nemo

Marlin

Dory

The Tank Gang

When you see these pictures say their names out loud:

Nemo

Marlin

Dory

The Tank Gang

In the fish tank, makes

friends with , who agree

to help him escape. But when

a pelican brings and

to the tank, they see playing

dead as part of his escape plan.

 leaves without realising that

 is alive!  help

into a drain, so he can swim

after .

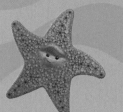

Left alone, forgets who she is and

why she's in Sydney, but when she sees

 it all comes back to her. reunites

 and , but gets caught in a fishing

net! gets into the net to tell all the

fish to swim down to the ocean floor.

When the net bursts open is proud

that he saved and 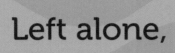 realises

that is just as brave and

capable as he is.

The End

Where's Nemo?

Nemo and his friends love to play
hide-and-seek amongst the coral.
Come and join them in the ocean!

1 Where is Nemo
hiding?

2 Can you point
to Jacques in the
picture?

Bruce's Tooth

Bruce needs Marlin and Nemo's help with a very sore tooth!

One day, Nemo and Marlin heard a dreadful groan.

"What's that?" asked Nemo.

"I don't know but it doesn't sound very friendly!" replied Marlin.

Nemo gasped when he saw a wall of very large, very sharp teeth in front of him.

"Thank goodness I found you!" cried Bruce, the shark. "I have killer toothache!"

"What can we do?" asked Nemo.

"Could you swim into my mouth and pull out my tooth?" Bruce asked.

"I've got an idea!" said Nemo, spotting a long strand of seaweed.

He told Marlin to wrap one end around Bruce's sore tooth and together, they pulled the other end with all their might. Bruce groaned, but the sore tooth didn't budge.

"COME ON EVERYONE!" called Nemo. "Bruce needs our help!"

Cautiously, all the fish on the reef came out of hiding and held the end of the seaweed.

"PULL!" yelled Marlin. Bruce winced, but the tooth stayed put.

"We need more help!" said Nemo.

Suddenly, there was a loud noise from above ...

FRRRRRRRRRRRRRR!

"It's a boat!" cried the crowd of fish, as they darted back into the coral.

Nemo swam up to the boat's propeller.

"Come back, Nemo!" cried Marlin. "That's too dangerous!"

"Trust me," replied Nemo, as he threw the end of the seaweed into the spinning blades. The propeller immediately yanked the sore tooth out of Bruce's mouth!

"The pain is gone!" cheered Bruce.

"We're glad we could help!" laughed Nemo and Marlin.

"I'll wear this to remind me of my helpful little pals," Bruce added, hanging the tooth and seaweed around his neck!

The End

Beaming Bruce

Bruce is thrilled that Nemo and his friends have cured his toothache!

Use your brightest pens to colour in this picture!

Who's Who?

See if you can match these sea creatures to the close-ups in the bubbles.

1

2

3

4

a　**b**　**c**　**d**

Marine Maze

Can you work out who will be able to swim through the maze to meet Peach, the starfish?

Nemo

Tad

FINISH

Pearl

Sheldon

50

Fishy Fun

Today the fish are learning the alphabet. Can you help them write the missing letters in the empty bubbles?

a   **d**   **f**   **g**

Answer: a b c d e f g

Can you spot five differences in picture 2? Colour Nemo each time you find one!

1

2

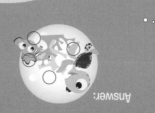

Answer:

Diver Distress

Can you help Marlin through the maze
to save his son before a diver catches him?
Watch out for the sharks!

How many
sharks did you
have to avoid?

52

Dory has encountered a shoal of fish that are making interesting shapes in the sea. Which shape looks like her friend Marlin?

1

2

3

4

5

Can you point to Sheldon?

Draw Nemo

See if you can draw a fantastic picture of Nemo, using the simple steps below to help you.

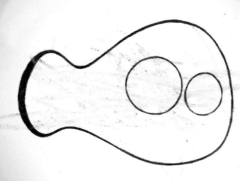

Step 1

Draw a fishy outline.

Step 2

Add the eyes, mouth and fins.

Step 3

Draw on Nemo's markings.

Step 4

Finally, add some colour.

Draw your Nemo here.

The Drop-Off

Nemo and his friends are playing a game at The Drop-Off. Are you brave enough to tackle these questions?

2 How many bubbles are there?

1 Who is swimming next to Nemo?

Pearl

M i a n i r

3 Rearrange the letters on the coral to find out who is looking for Nemo.

Nemo

4 Who is swimming the highest?

Tad

Sheldon

5 Look at this scary shadow. What type of creature do you think it is?

ANSWERS: 1. Tad, 2. 10 bubbles, 3. Marlin, 4. Nemo, 5. a shark.

57

Colour Dude!

This family of turtles is having fun with Dory. Add some cool colours to this scene.

Turtle Teasers

Dory and Marlin are riding the waves with the sea turtles. Answer these turtle-time teasers.

1 How many turtles are there? Trace the right answer.

3 4 5

2 Can you spot the turtle that is swimming upside down?

3 Circle the smallest turtle.

Cool Current

1 One day, Dory and Nemo were taking Squirt home from school along the East Australian Current. Nemo was very excited.

"Mr Ray told us that the current is so strong that it makes us swim ten times faster than normal," Nemo told Dory. "Isn't it cool!" cheered Squirt.

2 Suddenly, Squirt noticed an old shipwreck on the sea floor. "Wow! Look at that!" he gasped and swam down to explore the shipwreck.

3 "Hey, Squirt! Wait for me!" shouted Nemo, as he chased after him. "Who's Squirt?" asked Dory, forgetfully. Nemo smiled as the pair tried to catch up.

4 "Look at all the cool things down here," giggled Squirt. Soon, Squirt caught sight of an old diving helmet and swam inside to investigate.

5 But as Squirt swam inside, the grate suddenly snapped shut. "Help! I'm trapped!" cried Squirt, as Nemo and Dory rushed to help.

6 The two friends tried with all their strength to open the helmet but the grate was too heavy. "We're not strong enough!" strained Nemo.

7 Suddenly, Dory had an idea. "We're not strong enough but the current is!" she cried. Dory then threaded some rope through the grate.

8 The current was so strong that it pulled the rope tight and the front of the helmet sprang open. Nemo swam around excitedly.

"Thanks very much, Dory!" cried Squirt. "What for?" asked Dory, as they all happily rejoined the East Australian Current and headed for home.

About the story

1 Who went to explore the shipwreck?

2 Where did Squirt get trapped?

3 What did Nemo and Dory use to free Squirt?

4 What type of creature is Squirt?

5 What were Nemo, Dory and Squirt travelling along?

ANSWERS: 1. Squirt, Nemo and Dory, 2. in an old diving helmet, 3. a rope, 4. a sea turtle, 5. the East Australian Current.

Spot the Difference

Look closely at these pictures.
Can you find three differences between each pair?

1

2

Colour a shell for each difference you find.

3

ANSWERS:

63

Nemo's Friends

Nemo loves to spend time with his friends! Spend a little time with them too and solve these puzzles.

1

Join the dots to reveal one of Nemo's best friends!

Follow

2 · 3 · 4 · 5 · 6 · 7
1 · 37 · 8 · 9
36 · 10
35 · 11
12
13 · 15
34 · 14 · 16
32 · 33 · 18 · 17
31 · 28 · 25 · 19 · 20
30 · 29 · 22 · 21
27 · 26 · 24 · 23

a

b

2

Look closely at these pictures of Bruce. Can you spot the odd one out?

c

d

64

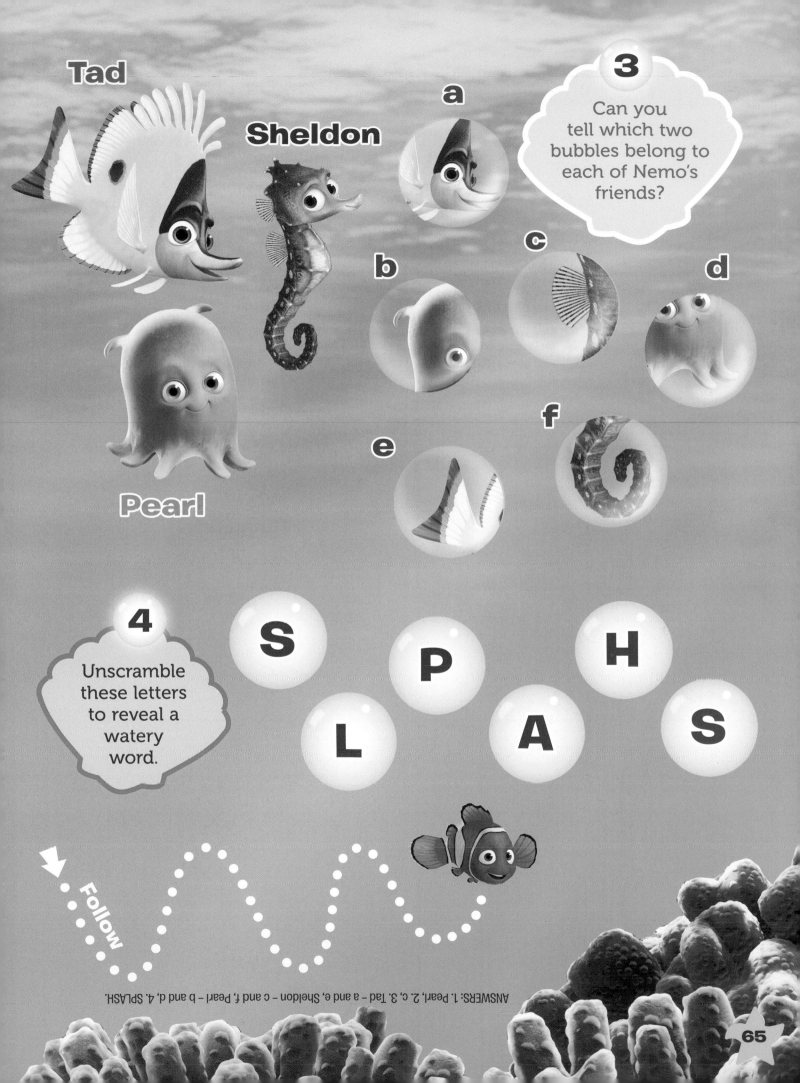

Tad

Sheldon

Pearl

a

b

c

d

e

f

3
Can you tell which two bubbles belong to each of Nemo's friends?

4
Unscramble these letters to reveal a watery word.

S P H

L A S

Follow

Odd Letter Out

Point to the odd letter
in each of these rows.

a N N N N M N

b E L E E E

c M M W M M

d O O O Q O

If you put together the first letter in each row,
what name appears? Write it below.

FINDING NEMO

Got your SWIM FINS?

CUT ALONG HERE

CUT ALONG HERE

Flying Colours

Nigel saves Marlin and Dory from hungry seagulls! Colour in the lucky friends.

1 What type of bird is Nigel?

☐ parrot

☐ pelican

2 Who is in Nigel's beak with Marlin?

69